Teachers Rock!

Todd Parr

Megan Tingley Books

LITTLE, BROWN AND COMPANY

New York   Boston

Also by Todd Parr

A complete list of Todd's books and more information can be found at **toddparr**.com.

This book was inspired by my love of teachers,
both those who encouraged me when I struggled in school
and those who support my books today.
Here's to all the great teachers in the world!

Love, Todd

About This Book

The art for this book was created on a drawing tablet using an iMac, starting with bold black lines and dropping in color with Adobe Photoshop. This book was edited by Megan Tingley and Allison Moore and designed by Saho Fujii. The text was set in Todd Parr's signature font. The production was supervised by Erika Schwartz, and the production editor was Marisa Finkelstein.

I love my teachers because...

They love coming to school, and

new things.

They help you find new talents.

Teachers read to you.

They play games with you, too.

Teachers are always willing to

help students in need.

Sometimes teachers make you laugh.

Sometimes they make you feel better.

Teachers let you share

all your favorite things.

O P Q R S T U V W X Y Z 1 2

Teachers make the classroom a great place to be.

make new friends.

of celebrations.

They take you on field trips.

Teachers love when your

families come to visit.

Teachers can be

just like you and me.

Teachers encourage you to try your best.

Most of all, they love to see you succeed!

Teachers are Very Special! 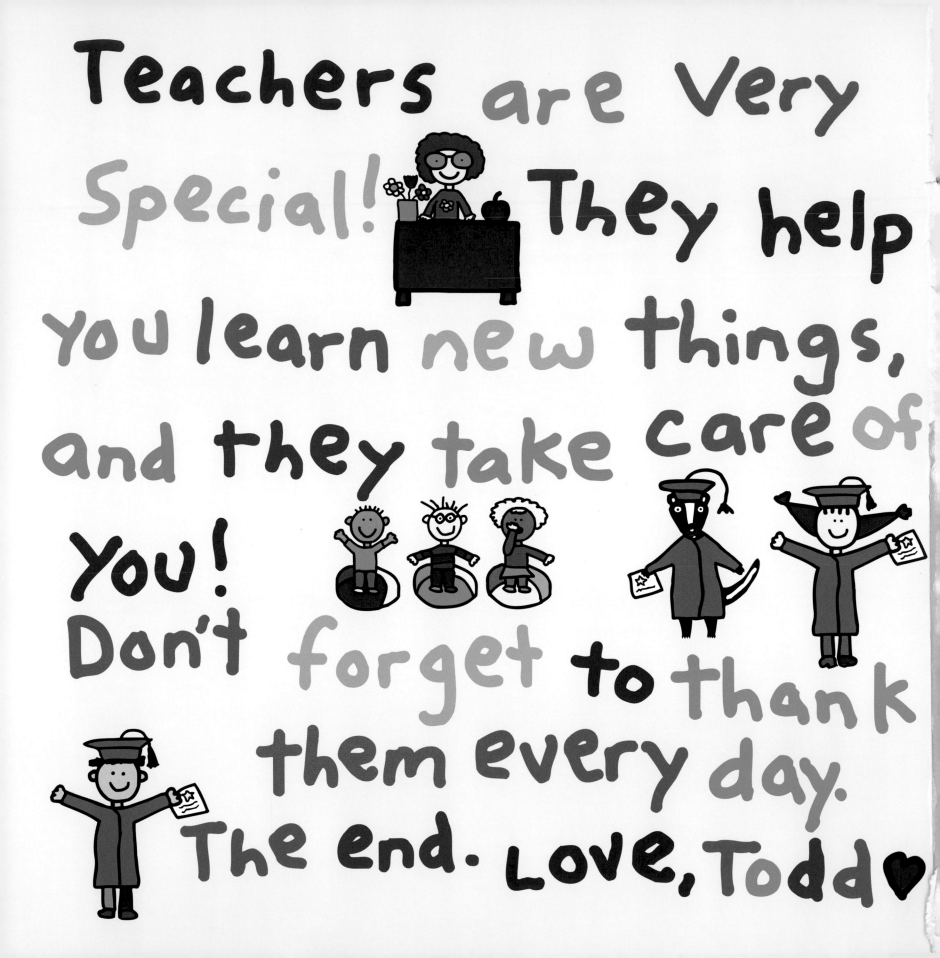 They help you learn new things, and they take care of You! Don't forget to thank them every day. The end. Love, Todd ♥